Sarah Cat Loves Cheese!
(Part Deux)

The Love Affair Goes On...

by CNC Ruggles

Illustrations by Cayci Woday

To order additional copies of this book, contact:
Xlibris LLC
1-888-795-4274
www.Xlibris.com
Orders@Xlibris.com

Sarah Cat Loves Cheese!
(Part Deux)

The Love Affair Goes On...

by CNC Ruggles

Illustrations by Cayci Woday

For some delicious cheese that is known as Ricotta
Sarah Cat would spend a fortune, and I mean a lotta!
The money she'd spend doesn't quite belong to her
But she would say to the bank teller,
"She won't mind, I am sure!"
Then she'd continue, "My Mistress has
told me what's hers is mine
So giving me all her money should certainly be fine!"
The teller would reply, "I can't close an account for a cat.
Besides, your name isn't on this
account, are you aware of that?"
Sarah Cat would then frown and say with a hiss
"Well, I've never heard of such an establishment as this!"

For any amount of Feta cheese
Sarah Cat would walk a hundred miles on her knees!
She wouldn't even care if the ground was hard as stone
As long as when she got there, the
Feta cheese was hers alone!
Even if someone tried to get Sarah Cat to share
She would growl and hiss and say, "I
really have none to spare!"
I tried to teach Sarah Cat the art of
sharing by watching "BARNEY"
But Sarah Cat just kept saying how that
dinosaur was full of blarney!
Now, understand, Sarah Cat would give you the
fur off her back, if you just said, "Please."
But if you asked her to share her cheese,
she'd say, "Ah, go tease some fleas!"

For a nice huge chunk of that cheese called Asiago
Sarah Cat would paint as well as Picasso!
She would travel around, appearing at art shows
With drawings and paintings of all of her cheese woes!
When somebody asked her what
her paintings were about
"I just can't get enough Asiago!" she'd most likely shout!
Eventually, I would find her traveling around Rome
So I'd say, "Sarah Cat, it is time to come home!"
Sarah Cat would look at me, as sad as could be
And say, "I think there is more cheese
on this side of the sea!"
I'd laugh and reply, "Sarah Cat, there is
plenty of cheese in America, as well
Besides, don't you think living in America is swell?!"
Then Sarah Cat would say, "Yes, America is great
But how much will it cost to send my
cheese portraits by freight?!"

9

For a great big piece of a cheese called Brie
Sarah Cat would climb to the top of the tallest tree!
She would climb so high till the ground she couldn't see
Then she'd come down fast, hollering, "Brie, Brie, Brie!"
When she got to the bottom and
stepped onto the ground
There her great big piece of Brie would be found!
She would eat her cheese with a great big smile
Then run back up the tree for what seemed like a mile!
Sarah Cat would come back down,
then hit the ground running
Yelling, "Last one by the pool misses out on the sunning!"
I'd say, "Sarah Cat, don't you steal my favorite place!"
She'd giggle and say, "I think it should
go to whoever wins this race!"

11

Whenever Sarah Cat eats her cheese called Gorgonzola
She likes to wash it down with at least two liters of cola!
At the end of this frenzy of eating and slurping
It seems there is always a whole lot of burping!
Whenever I would tell Sarah Cat that burping isn't polite
She'd always say, "Who has time for manners, when
you're thinking of cheese morning, noon, and night!"
I'd laugh and tell Sarah Cat, "You should
always try to be considerate and nice
Because you're one of the lucky kitties,
who's only food staple aren't mice!"
She'd reply, "I know, you are always
telling me things like that
But please cut me some slack, I'm just a little black cat!"

Sarah Cat always runs to the fridge when
I make my list to take to the store
And she'll ask, "Do we have enough String
cheese, or do you think we need more?"
I'll laugh and say, "Sarah Cat, I haven't
had a chance to check on that yet
But at the rate that you eat it, we're out, I'll bet!"
Sarah Cat will reply, "Yes, if I were a betting cat
I would certainly be doing some betting on that!"
Then I'll say, "I'm glad you don't use my
money for betting on cheese
If you did, before long, we'd be living
with my sister, Louise!"
Then Sarah Cat's eyes will light up as she asks,
"Doesn't your sister live by a store?
We would never run out of cheese, because
it would be so easy to get more!"
Then Sarah Cat will swoon till she
is practically on the floor
And she'll continue, "Wow, a store with cheese galore!
And, better yet, it's right next door!"

For a nice big hunk of that cheese called Velveeta
To the kitchen, Sarah Cat would beata her feeta!
She would fly into the kitchen as fast as you please
And she'd say, "Hey, I see you're cooking with cheese!"
I'd laugh and say, "Yes, without cheese,
this recipe you can't make!"
Then Sarah Cat would respond, "Well, I sure hope
you have enough, because I'm here for my take!"
Then I'd say, "You know, Sarah Cat,
sometimes you make cooking a chore!"
To which she would reply, "Well, if you're sure you
don't want to cook with that cheese anymore
You can always just pile it right here on the floor!"

On cold winter days when the sun won't show
And the cold, cold wind just continues to blow
Sarah Cat wouldn't care if it snowed enough to need skis
As long as she had plenty of cheese!
As a matter of fact, if she had cheese to eat
The cold and the snow could freeze her feet!
She would simply go inside and get warmed up
And ask for cheese when it's time for sup!
On cold winter nights, Sarah Cat
sleeps by the fire and dreams.
You can tell it is cheese she is dreaming of,
because her little black face, it just beams!
She rolls over on her back with her
tummy toward the ceiling
And she says, "Dreaming of cheese
gives me such a warm feeling!"

For a big, fat bowl of Parmesan cheese
A saber-toothed tiger, Sarah Cat would tease.
She would step on his toes while thumping his nose
And she would even pull his tail,
just to see how that goes!
Is there anything Sarah Cat won't do for some cheese?
If you know the answer to that, do tell me PLEASE!
I told Sarah Cat to stop risking her life
To which she replied, "Not eating
cheese is what brings me strife!
For cheese I would even bungee jump
and risk a thousand-foot fall!
I guess what I'm saying is, my love
for cheese isn't "SMALL"!"
I told Sarah Cat, "I do know what you mean.
Once I had a "BIG" love for a guy who
was tall, blonde, and lean!"
Sarah Cat laughed and asked, "Is this fella
you speak of still part of your heart?"
I replied, "Well, he's certainly still handsome, but
a thirty-year crush wouldn't really be smart!"

For one little piece of cheesecake
made with real cream cheese
Sarah Cat would head to the nearest prison,
and start handing out the keys!
When the warden and his men finally
got everyone back inside
He would probably tell Sarah Cat, "This
kind of thing I just can't abide!"
Sarah Cat would look up at him with
her innocent little eyes
And say, "Well, nobody ever told me that
those fellas weren't good guys!"
The warden would then feel pity for this little black cat
And say, "Okay, but I do hope never
again would you ever try that!"
Sarah Cat would cross her fingers
behind her back, then wink
Promising, "Never again, dear sir, and thank you
so much for not tossing me in the klink!"

Sarah Cat could eat cheese morning, noon, and night
If she wore any clothes they would surely be too tight!
Sarah Cat doesn't care because cheese is just so good
She wouldn't give it up, not even if she could!
I pity the poor fool who would try to tell her she should!
If I thought I could live with her, I guess maybe I would!
I tried telling Sarah Cat eating too
much cheese was bad to do
But she pretended not to hear me
and looked down at my shoe.
I smiled and asked, "Sarah Cat, are you listening to me?"
She responded, "Yes, but if you keep talking
that way, I most certainly will flee!"

When Sarah Cat found out the moon may be cheese
She said, "Quickly now, get me a rocket ship, please!
For a piece of cheese the size of the moon
There's really no way I could get there too soon!"
I believe for a piece of cheese that big
To China, Sarah Cat would attempt to dig!
Digging to China would make her
hungry, wouldn't you bet?
So most likely, she'd find out if the
restaurants had opened up yet!
If they had, she would go in and order cheese in a flash
And she would try to pay for the
cheese with a little cat cash
The server would say, "I don't know if we accept
that currency. Let me ask my boss, if you please!"
Sarah Cat would then frown and say, "Oh, golly geez!
I don't understand this language, Chinese!"

If Sarah Cat met the Man in the Moon
For his Green cheese she would surely swoon.
If he offered her some she would grab a spoon
And when she finished there'd be half a moon!
She would then take his hand and give it a squeeze
While saying, "Thank you, dear sir,
for that wonderful cheese!"
She then would say with a little cat laugh
"I guess I should go now. It seems I've
carved your moon in half!"
The Man in the Moon would then surely reply
"With your tummy that full, are you sure you can fly?!"
Sarah Cat would answer, "Oh, don't
worry about me, I'll be just fine!
As a matter of fact, when there is another
full moon, I'll be right back to dine!"

Back toward the earth herself she did hurdle
If Sarah Cat keeps eating cheese,
she will soon need a girdle!
She used to run fast and could climb like a squirrel
But now she can't even outrun a turtle!
If she keeps eating cheese at this very fast pace
She may even place last in a snail race!
However, if at the top of a tree a piece
of cheese Sarah Cat spies
We all know she would outrun a squirrel,
or even a crow as it flies!
Nothing could get that cheese quicker than Sarah Cat
Not a road runner, gazelle, or even a jet-propelled bat!

31

When Sarah Cat did return from space
For even more cheese, she still had a taste.
She thought to herself, to the center of
the earth, I really must scurry!
Then she thought, I must have more
cheese, and I must have it in a hurry!
Sarah Cat remembered someone once said the
center of the earth was a million degrees
So she thought, hey! If I get some bread, I just
might be able to have a grilled cheese!
I have heard that some would go
to middle earth for a ring
But I think it's safe to say that Sarah Cat would only
go there for cheese, like American or String!

For a delicious piece of Mozzarella
Sarah Cat would bow to an English fella
She'd say, "Dear fella, for a piece of that cheese
I would climb to the top of Big Ben with ease!"
She would then tell him something else to raise his brow
She'd say, "I jumped over the moon, not a cow!"
Then Sarah Cat would tell him her
Green cheese-eating story
And he would just think she was looking for glory!
This English fella would then say to Sarah Cat
"Do you really expect me to believe a story like that?!"

If you ever have a party, don't put Sarah
Cat in charge of the cheese
For Sarah Cat's motto is, "One for you, and ten for me"
So what Sarah Cat considers fair
can always make me laugh
Because what she takes for herself
is always far more than half!
As a matter of fact, if there is anyone else
in the room that may be wanting some
Sarah Cat will fake an injury and cry, "I
can't feel my legs! They're numb!"
While everyone runs to the phone to quickly call 9-1-1
Sarah Cat will reach for the cheese and
think, boy, are these people dumb!
When everyone finally realizes what Sarah Cat has done
Some will think, being fooled by a
cat, really isn't much fun!
But most will think, of this cheese, that
cat should be getting none!

37

I decided to take Sarah Cat to "Cheese
Addicts Anonymous" for help
They suggested breaking her addiction to
cheese by feeding her some kelp!
That is when my little Sarah Cat ran
out of the room with a yelp!
Once back in the car, Sarah Cat said with a frown
"I'd rather eat dirt than old seaweed, so
can we leave this crummy town?!"
On the way home I glanced over at Sarah Cat,
who was sitting in the passenger seat
What did I see? Sarah Cat covered in cheese
from her head to her little black feet!
She even had wedges of cheese
between her little kitty cat toes
So I did a quick U-Turn and said, "Back to
"Cheese Addicts Anonymous" we goes!"
Sarah Cat replied, "Okay, fine, we can go back
But there will be no seaweed for
this little cat that is black!
Let's agree on that on this very day
So I won't have to contact the "ASPCA"!"

When Sarah Cat's cheese-eating day is finally done
She will lie down and dream of all
the cheese prizes she's won.
She will dream she has won a trip to the Island of Cheese
Where everything is cheese, even the trees!
Sarah Cat will climb a tree and lie down on a limb
She will munch on the leaves and the
bark till the tree is quite trim!
By the time Sarah Cat finally gets done
The tree that once stood ten feet tall will stand only one!
It is a good thing it is only a dream
Because if Sarah Cat ever eats nine feet
of cheese, the solution is plain
The only way to move her will be with a crane!
Tomorrow Sarah Cat will begin her
quest for cheese all over again
But tonight she goes to sleep, and upon
her face, is a cheese-eating grin
So this is the perfect time to say
of this story, "THE END!"

CPSIA information can be obtained at www.ICGtesting.com
Printed in the USA
LVIW01n1424250215
428331LV00016B/95